Red Robin Books is an imprint of Corner To Learn Limited

Published by
Corner To Learn Limited
Willow Cottage • 26 Purton Stoke
Swindon • Wiltshire SN5 4JF • UK

ISBN: 978-1-905434-29-9

First published in the UK 2004
New edition published in the UK 2009
Text © Neil Griffiths 2004
Illustrations © Vicki Leigh 2004

Design by
David Rose

Printed in China by
PrintWORKS

The Scarecrow
Who Didn't Scare

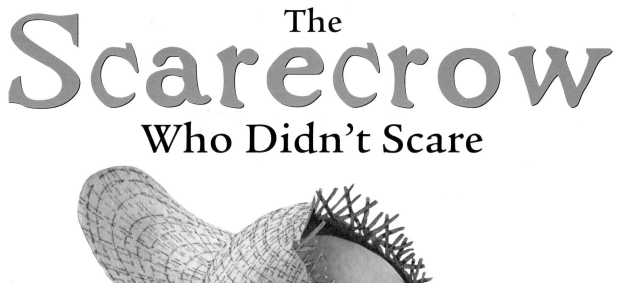

Neil Griffiths

Illustrated by Vicki Leigh

Farmer Wallace had
been very busy making
this year's scarecrow.

At last he had found a use for his wedding day suit that no longer fitted him ...

... an old pair of brown boots with holes in the toes he hadn't worn for years ...

... and some bright green gardening gloves he had never liked.

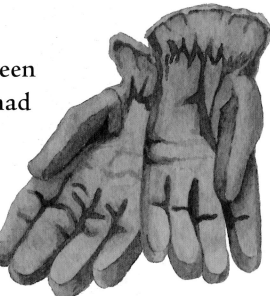

Mrs Wallace had also donated one of her sunhats that had been chewed by the dog.

The farmer felt sure it would do a good job as he pushed its pole deep into the newly ploughed field.

As spring arrived, the scarecrow tried its hardest to keep the birds away from the newly planted seed.

But they took no notice and ate and ate until they were full!

Several weeks later, it did all that it
could to frighten the rabbits too ...

... but they weren't frightened
at all and greedily ate the
tender growing shoots.

As summer arrived, it tried to scare the mice from the ripening corn, but they weren't scared either and scampered up the tall golden stalks and nibbled endlessly.

When the farmer returned in late summer to harvest his field he could scarcely believe his eyes!

All that remained were a few clumps of wheat hardly worth harvesting at all.

He was so angry,
that he pulled
the scarecrow
from the ground
and threw it into
the hedge nearby.

There it lay,
sad and alone
throughout
the autumn.

The winter that followed was very cold indeed.
The ground was frozen hard, icicles hung from the
branches and frost covered the hedges for days.

The wind blew wildly and
the air became colder and colder.

One by one the woodland creatures came out of hiding in search of warmth.

They sat shivering beneath the scarecrow, who was so pleased to see them as it had been very lonely.

It soon forgot how troublesome they had all been and invited them to cuddle up for warmth in its straw stuffing.

The birds nestled snugly in its hat ...

... the rabbits climbed into each cosy jacket pocket ...

... and the mice made themselves comfortable
in the old brown boots, all pleased
to be out of the bitter cold.

As spring arrived, the farmer returned to plant new seed and decided to give the scarecrow one more chance, as he had been too busy to make a new one.

In return for the scarecrow's kindness ...

... the birds ate not one
newly planted seed ...

... the rabbits left the
green shoots to grow ...

... and the mice did not
climb the golden stalks
in search of corn.

As late summer arrived,
the farmer was rewarded
with a bumper harvest,
the best he had ever had!

The farmer smiled proudly at the scarecrow.
The scarecrow smiled back and was secretly looking forward
to winter when the woodland creatures would
return again and keep it company.

The End

Neil Griffiths is a former Primary School headteacher and the creator of the internationally-acclaimed and award-winning Storysack® concept. He has a passion for children's literature and his many books feature strong storylines, memorable characters, enchanting language, and arresting illustrations.

Neil loves to tell a story and storytime with him is a rare and highly entertaining event as he magically draws his audience into his storyworlds. For more information on Neil's storytime sessions, inspirational training workshops or his many other books, visit his website at: **www.redrobinbooks.com**.

Other books by Neil Griffiths

www.redrobinbooks.com